ISBN: 0692889914
ISBN 13: 9780692889916

Prologue

There is no beginning; each story starts long before the reader enters. This one started in a small town or it started at a government facility; maybe the beginning was the chemical spill that turned the town into zombies and took all the colors. Either way, you entered after both, this book takes place even later. It's the next chapter.

We should make one thing clear, there is a progression to Zombiehood. First it's all brains and eating things but after that it calms down a little bit. Eat enough meat and you can run around and talk like a normal kid.

Caleb and the town, which was called Eidolon, were brainless at first but they figured it out. After awhile the kids started going back to school and the parents went back to work, there wasn't any color in the town but they started to think that was normal. It wasn't until Caleb started painting everything that zombies like the Mayor and his teacher started throwing a fit. Eventually Caleb painted the whole town and everyone realized how beautiful the colors were. It's been a tradition to paint the town with new colors ever since then and their bodies have slowly gotten their color back although they still remain zombies.

That's pretty close to where we pick up…

chapter 1

The air was full of confetti. Colors were raining down on Caleb's
head as he was paraded around the town square on his father's
shoulders. He was so happy the town had come to love colors.
No more drab black and white; a new world had been opened
up to them, and Caleb was responsible.

"Caleb, we love you!" the neighbor yelled.

"You're the coolest," said a friend from school.

Everyone was dancing and celebrating. As he looked around, one man gave him a trophy, another a high five. Finally Nola, a girl from school he played with sometimes, pushed through the crowd with something in her hands. She reached up as high as her little zombie arms could reach, and Caleb took the stuffed animal.

It was a unicorn so white it almost seemed to glow. Caleb studied the gift with a smile, but as he looked up to thank the girl, she was gone. So were his dad, the town square and everyone who had just been there. Instead, all around were small yellow flowers and a Unicorn that had grown much larger than the size of his hand.

"You lost your big toe," the Unicorn remarked as he circled the little zombie boy.

Caleb, surprised, looked down and realized it was true. He began searching through the grass and flowers but couldn't find his toe.

Meanwhile, the unicorn had walked to the edge of the woods. "It's right here!" he called to Caleb.

As Caleb approached, the unicorn moved a branch out of the way, and beneath it was an average-sized child zombie toe, slightly blue and white, bruised at the joint and stinking of dirty feet. Caleb sat down and began trying to reattach it, first putting it on upside down, then backward. No matter how hard he tried, it wouldn't go back in place. Finally, he looked up at the unicorn in frustration and began to cry.

"What about flying?" the Unicorn asked.

"I've always wanted to," Caleb said through a sob. As he began floating above the ground, he forgot about his missing toe. "Have you ever wanted to be an animal?" the Unicorn continued.

"Sometimes, I want to be a lion," Caleb replied, as he softly landed on the ground and transformed into a lion.

Nothing seemed strange to Caleb until the unicorn began walking away and mumbling something.

"What did you say?" Caleb called after him,

"It's time to wake up," the Unicorn whispered.

"What did you say?" Caleb called after him,

The Unicorn turned around. "It's time to wake up, Caleb."

"Caleb, it's time to wake up," he heard again.

Then, "Caleb!" he heard his mom yell. "It's time to wake up!"

chapter 2

That wasn't all his mom had to say, though. "Caleb, get your carcass out of that bed!" he heard her say as she was thumping up the stairs. "Do you know what day it is?"

Instantly Caleb knew. It was Friday, and the festival was tomorrow. Everyone in town would be at the square for one reason: to celebrate the colors Caleb had spread over the town. Even though it would be three years ago tomorrow, he could still see the crowd, feel the joy of being lifted above his father's head. He couldn't contain his excitement. Quickly he jumped out of bed, looked at his sleeping dog Max and began rubbing him all over.

"Wake up, you old sleepy head, we have to get ready for the fair tomorrow."

Max jumped around his legs as Caleb pulled on his cleanest dirty pants and ran downstairs for breakfast.

Everything seemed normal as he passed his mom on the stairs, but it quickly devolved into a funny sort of day.

First, Caleb stubbed his toe as he came around the couch. Images of the dream last night flashed through his mind, but he shook it off and devoured his cereal. Next, he fell on the playground and had to visit the nurse, but she was out of band-aids.

"The nurse, out of band-aids? What is going on today?" Caleb asked himself.

At lunch they were out of apple slices, he saw Nola take the last pack. His pencil broke in class and he didn't have another one, and his shoelace broke, too. Finally, he missed the bus home because he was talking to his friends.

As Caleb walked home, he realized he was exhausted and in a grumpy mood.

After such a cool dream and with such an exciting day tomorrow, he wondered, "how could it have gone so wrong?"

The only thing that kept him going was the excitement for the fair tomorrow.

At dinner he was quiet and ate without playing with his food. When his mom finally said it was time for bed, Caleb had already brushed his teeth and put on his jammies. Like every other night, his mom and dad came in to read him a bedtime story, but Caleb was too tired. He fell asleep thinking about seeing everyone tomorrow and wondering what the city had planned for him.

5

chapter 3

The air was full of confetti. Colors were raining down on Caleb's head as the crowd paraded around the town square, Caleb on his father's shoulders, grinning. He was so happy the town had come to love colors. No more drab black and white; a new world had been opened up to them, and Caleb had discovered it.

"Caleb, we love you!" the neighbor yelled.

"You're the coolest," said a friend from school.

Everyone was dancing and celebrating. Caleb was so happy. As he looked around, one man gave him a trophy, another a high five. Finally Nola, a girl from school he played with sometimes, pushed through the crowd with something in her hands. She reached up as high as her little zombie arms could reach, and Caleb took the stuffed animal.

It was a white unicorn, Caleb studied the gift. It seemed oddly familiar but something was wrong. The unicorn was dull and matted. The normally bright mane was drab and tangled, and the tail was gray. Caleb looked at it and was confused. Suddenly, a balloon bounced off his head and he looked up again.

There were balloons everywhere. Most of the crowd had stopped cheering and were busy showing each other their fancy bright clothes and plaid shirts. Finally, Caleb tapped his dad's shoulder and asked to be let down. Nola and his friend from class, Jake, ran off with Max on their heels to find somewhere to play.

"Where should we go?" Caleb asked.

"Let's go to the school," Nola suggested.

"The park!" Jake, a boy from Caleb's class, yelled.

"The park, the park," the three started chanting.

"Woof," Max chimed in agreement.

chapter 4

It was summer, and the kids didn't have school until next month, so they didn't notice that the sun was beginning to set. Nola immediately ran over and climbed up the monkey bars, and Jake began climbing up the slide, but Caleb stopped at the edge of the playground.

He couldn't believe what he was seeing. Was it a trick? Maybe a storm was coming in or the clouds were hanging low, but the edge of town was shrouded in a dense, gray fog. As Caleb watched, it was slowly coming closer. He wasn't sure, but it looked like the trees turned gray, too. The color was slowly fading up the trunk and spreading to the leaves, one branch at a time.

Nola and Jake were still playing when they heard Caleb yell, "Come look at this."

Nola looked while hanging upside-down, but she didn't notice, and Jake was halfway up a slide tunnel.

Caleb yelled, "Guys! Come look at this."

Jake popped out of the tunnel and came running down the play set, catching the fire pole on his way down and bumping into Caleb.

"What is it?" Jake asked, looking at the fog, "Nola, come over here."

Caleb and Jake were staring as Nola slowly came up to them.

"I don't like it," she said uneasy. "Maybe we should go home."

"Are you kidding me?" Jake responded. "It's nothing but fog."

"I don't know," disagreed Caleb. "We should go find our parents."

Max was pacing nervously.

"You guys are silly," Jake boasted. "I'll show you, it's nothing."

Jake started walking toward the fog, acting brave, but Max got more and more nervous until he finally started barking and jumping on Caleb.

"Max, stay down," Caleb said, eyes fixed on Jake the whole time.

Finally, Max sat down but couldn't sit still. He was watching Jake as he passed into the fog.

"See, guys?" Jake turned around and yelled. "It's just fog."

Something strange was happening, though. The fog started to move around Jake. It was slow at first, but it started moving faster, swirling into a circle around him.

"Help!" Jake cried.

"Get out of there," yelled Caleb, as he started running toward him.

Jake began to run towards Caleb, screaming. The fog was still swirling around him as he reached out his hand. Caleb grabbed it and began to pull, but the fog held on. Nola ran over and grabbed Jake's arm. It was cold. She grabbed on and pulled with all her might.

"Max, help!" Caleb yelled.

Max ran up, bit Jake's sleeve and started to pull. With a final effort they pulled him out and a clap of thunder burst overhead.

It seemed as if all of the sound had been sucked out of the world, and the kids' ears were ringing. Caleb and Nola were looking at Jake with their mouths open. Max smelled Jake's leg and began growling softly. As they watched him, the last wisps of fog were rising from around him. Starting at his feet, the color faded from his jeans, then his shirt, until Caleb and Nola saw the green come out of Jake's eyes and he let out a soft gasp.

Jake didn't move. His eyes didn't notice Caleb's hand waving in front of his face or Nola yelling about the color of his clothes. Jake was drooling a little, and he was black and white. Slowly, Caleb realized Jake was back to being a full-blown mindless zombie.

Chapter 5

"Wake up, wake up, wake up," Caleb repeated as he shook Jake by the shoulder.

"He doesn't look right," Nola said, backing away, "I'm scared."

Max was still growling and circling the kids when Jake seemed to recognize that something was happening around him. His glassy eyes looked straight at Caleb.

"Bah-rains," he mumbled, slowly taking a step forward.

Max immediately started going crazy. He was barking at the top of his lungs and nipping at Caleb's ankle. Nola and Caleb were holding hands now and backing away from Jake.

"Bah-rains," Jake said again as he stumbled on the sand.

He took another step and lunged for Nola.

"Ahhhh!" she cried, almost losing her balance.

Caleb quickly helped her stand up as Jake continued to come towards them. He was slow and dragging his feet; his right arm was limp, and he acted like it was too heavy. After one last attempt at grabbing Caleb, Jake tripped and began writhing in the sand.

"Max, come on. We gotta go," Caleb said, as he started pulling Nola's arm. "We need to find my parents."

chapter 6

As Caleb, Nola and Max started running, they could see that the fog had grown. It now circled the whole town: the sun was blocked, but the town glowed with a flat, gray light. The streetlights were turning on along the streets as the kids wove their way back to the town square. Down one street, a left at the next, two blocks down and a right and they would be there. That's what they thought, anyway.

As they came around the final corner, they stopped dead in their tracks. The square was empty. Except for a few pieces of trash on the ground, it was as if the festival had never happened.

"Where is everybody?" Nola asked.

"Come on," Caleb replied.

He led her to the center of the square. After spinning a slow circle, Caleb pointed to an alley.

"I see someone," he said, and took off towards a gap between the buildings.

Nola was a step behind him but following fast. As they came to the alley, they could just see someone going around the corner and out of sight. Quickly they ran down the alley, and as they came around the corner, they found themselves staring at the mayor.

The mayor was hunched over a garbage can. With stiff arms he was throwing paper and boxes out of the way. Caleb was inching closer when the mayor found something—a rat hiding at the bottom of the dumpster. With surprising speed, the mayor grabbed the rat. He was straightening up when Nola accidently kicked a tin can.

Caleb's eyes looked up, only to be met by the mayor's cold gray eyes. There was no sparkle, but they focused on Caleb, and the mayor started to move forward.

"Run!" Nola cried.

chapter 7

Caleb ran back towards Nola and then around the building. They were almost out of the alley when a dark figure appeared at the entrance. It was like a cloud, billowing large behind a dark shape and spiraling out of it. Caleb and Nola froze. The monster didn't move, but they could see its eyes, white and glowing.

For what seemed like forever they stared at each other, neither moving nor making a sound, when behind Nola and Caleb came a crash of boxes being kicked and a loud groan as the mayor fell down.

The monster rushed forward, the cloud trailing behind and filling the alley. Max was the first to move, but Caleb and Nola turned to run as well. It was too late, though. The monster was on them.

Nola and Caleb were holding hands as Caleb followed Max inside a doorway, but as the cloud rushed past, Nola was swept away with a quick yelp. Caleb ran out the door only to see the plume racing over the town and spiraling into the clouds.

chapter 8

Caleb was stunned, frozen. He couldn't believe what had just happened. His mind was racing, but he was staring blankly at the spot of sky where Nola and the monster disappeared.

"Did that just happen?" he asked himself. "What am I going to do?"

He was so preoccupied, he didn't notice that the mayor had pushed the trash can off and was starting to get up. Max noticed and began barking, but Caleb didn't hear it. When the mayor got up and started looking around, Caleb didn't notice. When the mayor saw him, he didn't notice. He didn't even notice when the mayor started limping toward him.

Max wasn't a trained attack dog, but he was scared and knew he wouldn't let anything happen to Caleb. As the mayor inched closer, Max exploded and started running in circles around the mayor, trying to distract him, to trip him, anything to stop his slow approach. Finally, as Caleb was almost within arm's reach, Max jumped on the mayor from behind, forcing him to stumble on the trash can again and fall flat on his face onto the concrete.

Caleb snapped out of his daze, looked at the mayor, who was noticeably closer then he had been, and realized what had happened.

"Thanks boy, come on. We gotta find mom and dad," Caleb said with determination.

The two took off running back towards their house, hoping there wouldn't be any other surprises and that someone could help.

chapter 9

They ran through the town square, where there were now a few zombies he recognized. He told Max they should steer clear of everyone until they got home.

It shouldn't have been very far, a couple of blocks, but every time they avoided a mob of zombies, it added another block or building to go around. Finally, Caleb stopped, out of breath and doubled over

"Hold on, Max," Caleb said, panting. "This isn't working," he gasped. "The monster is trying to stop us from getting home. What can we do?"

Max looked at him and tilted his head with a confused look on his face.

"Well, that's helpful," Caleb exclaimed as his frustration grew. "Let's try going through the library."

"Woof," Max replied.

Surprisingly, the path to the library was clear. It sat in the middle of the block at the end of Fir Street with Second Street running directly in front of it, making a "T." As they ran toward it, each street they crossed had zombies coming up the block towards them. Max looked at Caleb and saw the concern on his face, but Fir was clear, so they kept running.

As they crossed Second, two groups of zombies were stepping onto Fir. They were closing off the street, Caleb realized. The only thing between them and the library was the lawn and a couple of steps, but the zombies were getting closer.

"Max!" Caleb yelled as he made one last effort to sprint between the groups.

They just barely made it through, and Caleb slammed the glass door behind them and locked it as fast as he could.

As Caleb opened his eyes in relief, he was terrified at what he saw. Standing in the center of the big entrance room was Jake, gray as a snail, standing stark still with a dark figure directly behind him, grinning from ear to ear.

"Hello Caleb. How are you today? Do you like what I've done with your town?" Jake asked.

"Jake, get away from him" Caleb said.

"Oh, Jake can't hear you," the monster said. "My name is Eniko, and I'm borrowing Jake's voice. What do you think, does it suit me?"

"No, you're evil. Leave him alone!" Caleb said.

Eidolon Library

"It seems a little high for me, but I think I'll keep it for a while," Eniko continued. "Besides, without it we couldn't have this lovely conversation. You were going to ask me a question?"

"Why are you doing this?" Caleb said.

"That was it. I am the forgotten one, the one without color. But 'why' isn't the interesting question, it's 'how' am I doing it. That's what you should ask me." Eniko paused, but Caleb only glared at him.

The zombies outside had reached the door, and it was starting to rattle behind him.

"You see, what I do is get inside their souls and take the color back. Haven't you noticed that there is more to the color than just a pretty tree or a fancy shirt? The color helped bring them back to humanity. It gave them hope and showed them that even though they might lose the occasional fingernail or patch of hair, they didn't have to eat brains all the time."

Caleb started to move away from the door. It was starting to bulge, but he didn't want to get any closer to Eniko. Max stayed by his side as they stepped in front of the information desk. As Eniko continued, he matched Caleb's steps, making sure to stay right in front of him.

"But this new world you helped show them wasn't good for me. I was still black and white. I didn't have humanity to come back to. Don't you see, I liked it that way? When you were black and white, we were the same. I belonged."

"You don't belong here," Caleb spat. "I'm going to beat you. My parents will help figure this out."

Eniko's mouth moved, but Jake's head fell back and a terrible laugh came out of him.

"Your parents?" Eniko scoffed. "They won't be able to help you. This is my world now."

The two continued to walk in opposite directions until Eniko and Jake were standing in front of the big double doors. Outside, the zombies were crowding around and pressing into each other. They wanted in.

"I am the future. I will be part of your town again," Eniko said as his voice grew louder. "There is no escape from me. I will take the ones you love and shatter your pretty little dreams."
Eniko had started yelling now, and Jake's voice cracked under the strain.

"There is no escaping the fog. We are everywhere."

Eniko ended with emphasis, and as he did, the doors broke open. The monster burst into a cloud of smoke, and the zombie horde rushed at Caleb, Jake leading the way.

chapter 10

Max and Caleb started running through the library, but Jake and the zombies were close behind them, so they headed through the aisles. Max's tail hit a stack of books as they ran. That gave Caleb a good idea, and he started pulling books down, but every time he turned around, Jake was still there. A few zombies in the front tripped, causing a dog pile, and the group finally fell behind, but Jake was still keeping pace and the smoke filled the room.

After a series of twists and turns, they lost Jake and hid behind a cart stacked with books. Caleb and Max were both panting when Caleb looked down at Max and said, "The smoke is getting thicker. We have to get out of here."

There were no lights on, and by now the air was thick and black. All they could see was a red glow coming from an exit sign, but they could hear the zombies stumbling around, bumping into the shelves and knocking things over.

Max was whimpering quietly when Caleb said, "Okay, on three we run for it."

They couldn't see but heard something getting closer. In the aisle behind them, books were being knocked off a shelf.

"One."

The sound of books hitting the floor was coming toward them.

"Two."

A zombie had come into the open but couldn't see them because of the cart.

"THREE!" Caleb yelled and took off toward the red glow.

At the same time, the zombie saw them and started chasing them. As they hit the door, it burst open, but the zombie dived forward and grabbed Max, who yelped and was pinned down.

Caleb turned around to see Jake and Max biting each other on the ground. He ran back and kicked at Jake, but it didn't matter. Jake had a hold on Max and wasn't letting go. Caleb pulled at Jake's arms, which felt like they were locked around the dog. Caleb was frantically pulling at Jake as he began to cry.

Yelling at Jake, he said, "Let go! He's my best friend!" Tears were running down his face.

But Jake only looked up at him and smiled the same smile Caleb had seen on Eniko.

"I want everything you love," Jake said before finally releasing Max.

The last thing Caleb saw was Jake smiling as the zombie horde swarmed around him and the door slammed shut.

23

Chapter 11

Caleb sat gasping against the back wall and was drying his face when he noticed Max licking at his back leg.

"Come here, boy," he called to the dog.

Max limped over, and Caleb could see he was missing a large piece of his left thigh.

"Argh, that monster!" Caleb said angrily. "We have to get this fixed up, or you'll never make it back to the house."

Max started licking his wound again while Caleb thought about what to do next. Caleb hadn't noticed that the area around the wound was already losing its color, but Max could feel that something was different. He quietly came face to face with Caleb and started licking his face softly.

"I need to nurse you back to health," Caleb pondered as he hugged the dog. "That's it! The school is on the way. We can stop there and get you fixed up and then go get help from mom and dad. What a great idea, Max."

Caleb got up and started walking around the building towards the school. It was only a couple of blocks, but he quickly noticed that Max was having a hard time keeping up. After the first block Caleb knelt down and waited for Max to catch up.

"I know it hurts, boy, but we have to keep going," he said.

By the time they got to the school, Max was barely able to make it up the stairs. When they got inside, it was eerily quiet, and Caleb got a bad feeling.

"We have to be stealthy. We're on a mission, and we don't know if there are any zombies in here," he said to Max.

Max whimpered softly and tucked his tail between his legs. Caleb looked down and noticed that Max's whole leg was now gray.

"We have to hurry," he thought.

Cha pter 12

Silently they walked down the empty halls. Caleb was crouched down, but he looked into the rooms as they passed to be sure they wouldn't be surprised. Inside was nothing but empty desks and old drawings from the students that were slowly losing their color.

As they came around the corner, Max let out a snarl.

"Shh," Caleb whispered. "I hear it too."

Somewhere down the hall, they could hear scratching coming from one of the rooms. They passed the first set of rooms, but they were empty. As they sneaked past Caleb's classroom, they could hear the sound coming from behind the door. Caleb had his back to the door but slowly turned around and peeked inside.

"Ms. Alexander's in there," he mouthed to Max.

He peered into the room again and saw that she was standing at the chalkboard. As he watched, she made a big circle, then a smaller one inside of it, then began aimlessly scribbling until she was scratching a notch with her fingernail.

Caleb motioned to Max, "Come on, we're almost there."

By the time they reached the nurse's office, Caleb was sweating with nervousness. They quickly slipped inside and closed the door.

Inside it was dark, but the moon shone just enough that Caleb could see around the room. He could see the light reflecting off the glass on the door to the principal's office, the white curtains that led to the back where kids laid down if they didn't feel well, and the cabinets that the nurse kept all her things in.

He was thinking about every time he had visited, from the time he sprained his ankle on the playground to the time he got a fever and had to wait for his parents, trying to remember where the nurse kept things. He spoke aloud as he moved about the room.

"She keeps the bandages over here," he said as he opened a cabinet. "Here they are. Come here, Max, let me wrap up your leg."

Max whimpered but wouldn't let Caleb come near.

"What is it?" Caleb asked, "Alcohol! That's it, Max, you're a genius. But she's never used anything like that on me."

Max lay down on the center of the room while Caleb searched. He went around the room opening and closing drawers and cabinets. After the first two failed attempts he started moving faster and forgot he need to keep quiet, until he eventually slammed a cupboard and startled himself.

"Where is it?" he asked aloud.

Out of the corner of his eye he saw a glass-front cupboard. Inside it were peroxide, swabs and rubbing alcohol.

"Finally," Caleb said as he grabbed the bottle and knelt down beside Max.

The color had almost gone completely out of Max, but his eyes lit up as Caleb poured the clear liquid on his leg. With a start, Max stood up and faced Caleb.

"It's okay Max, lie down."

But Max didn't lie down; he stared straight ahead and slowly curled his lip. It was small at first but grew until his full teeth were bared. Caleb wasn't usually scared of his best friend, but it made him nervous.

"What is it?" he asked.

Max started to growl quietly.

"Max, no," Caleb said in a stern voice, "Ms. Alexander will hear you."

chapter 13

Suddenly, Caleb heard the door behind him creaking. Max had lowered his head and was growling with his full throat. Caleb stood up and turned around to see the Principal standing in the doorway, a shadow in the darkness.

"Max, we have to go," Caleb said as he started to step towards the other door while keeping his eyes on the Principal.

Max was following slowly and the Principal was walking towards him. Caleb was still watching the Principal as he opened the door behind him.

"Come on, WE HAVE TO GO."

But Max kept the same steady pace and was growling all the while. The Principal came up beside him and knelt down, petting the dog between the shoulders.

"MAX!" Caleb yelled.

"I told you I would come for him," the Principal said.

Caleb instantly recognized Eniko's voice.

"Are you hungry?" the Principal asked Max. "Go get him, then."

Caleb's eyes were wide in disbelief as the Principal patted Max on the rump and pushed him forward. He looked into Max's eyes but saw only darkness and hunger. Max barked and lunged forward. Caleb fell backwards through the door as Max kept coming.

Out in the hall, Caleb slipped on the tile while trying to get to his feet. He had started crying and was scooting backwards as fast as he could. Max burst through the opening and slammed into the lockers on the other side of the hall. Caleb finally reached his feet but was still calling to the dog.

"Max, you can't do this," he cried.

Max couldn't get up. His leg kept falling out from under him, but he continued inching towards Caleb.

"I need you, Max. Stop it."

But the dog kept coming. Foam had worked up around his mouth, and he was snarling wildly.

"Max, I can't leave you."

Finally, the Principal came out of the office and grabbed Max's collar.

"Better run and find mommy and daddy before you get bit," he said to Caleb. "Besides, Ms. Alexander heard the commotion, and pretty soon you won't have anywhere to go."

Caleb took off running. Tears were streaming down his face as he made his way through the halls. Finally, he burst out of the door, only to be soaked by the pouring rain that had started. He didn't care, though—he had to find his parents and fix this.

chapter 14

Caleb ran wildly though the streets toward his house until he thought his lungs would burst. He finally collapsed on his lawn and sobbed while the rain continued to fall.

It took him a minute to catch his breath, but when he did, the downpour had become a drizzle and he could see the first signs of morning coming over the sky.

Caleb had never stayed up all night and felt a small bit of excitement at the idea. It was short-lived, though, because immediately he noticed that the usual yellows were replaced by shades of gray.

He stood up and wiped his face, making his way toward the house.

"Mom, Dad," he called as he walked through the door.

The house was silent, but Caleb could see that the light in the kitchen was on. He crept around the corner, expecting the worst, but hoping for the best. To his relief, both of his parents were there.

"Mom, they got Max," Caleb said as he started to cry again.

"Why are you home so late?" Caleb's mom replied. "We've been worried sick about you."

Caleb walked over and wiped his face on her shirt.

"Mom, did you hear me? Max is gone." Caleb said. "Something's happening to the town. There's a monster."

"Don't be silly. Things are the way they are supposed to be," his mom said.

She was facing the window. Caleb stood back in alarm.

"Why are you so calm?" Caleb screamed. "Max is gone."

He grabbed his dad's arm and was tugging at his sleeve.

"You have to help me fix this," Caleb cried. "I don't know what to do."

He was pulling at his dad's arm when he slipped. The fall brought his father down on top of him. As Caleb looked up, he was horrified to see his father's face pale and gray.

"We know all about Max," Caleb's dad said, while lifting himself off the floor. "Max is with us now."

chapter 15

Behind Caleb's dad a figure was slowly taking shape. There was a familiar smile forming and it was wrapping around his dad's shoulder. The same smile Jake had had while he laughed as Caleb ran out of the library. This time was different, though. Caleb had had enough. This was too much. Eniko had gone too far.

"You give me my parents back," Caleb shouted at his dad. "Give me back my town!"

At the last syllable the smile disappeared into a cloud of smoke.

"But Caleb, you know I can't do that," came a voice from behind him.

Caleb spun around, startled. His eyes had been fierce while looking at the familiar face of his dad, but the look melted away at the sight of the monster standing before him. Caleb had not seen Eniko like this before—part child, part smoke, looming with his toothy grin.

"This is the way it's supposed to be, Caleb," he continued. "We were the best of friends before, but you forgot about me. Left me discarded that day you found the paint cans in the garage. I only want to be your friend, Caleb."

"You are a monster," Caleb spat. "I could never be your friend." As Caleb spoke, Eniko began to get angry.

"Caleb," he said gritting his teeth. "You always were so much fun to play with. Why can't we be like that again? Why can't we start over?"

"You have taken everything from me. We were mindless zombies after the accident and I helped bring us back. Things were almost normal until you ruined everything. I hate you!"

Eniko was puffing by now, and with each heavy breath, the kitchen filled more and more with smoke. His breath was a black that no color could escape. It withered the hair on Caleb's head and turned his shirt to an ashen gray for a moment. As Eniko began to take another breath, Caleb turned with fear on his face and ran out of the kitchen.

He could hear the chairs being knocked over and glass breaking, but he wasn't going to look back. He darted through the hall and up the stairs, running into his room and slamming the door.

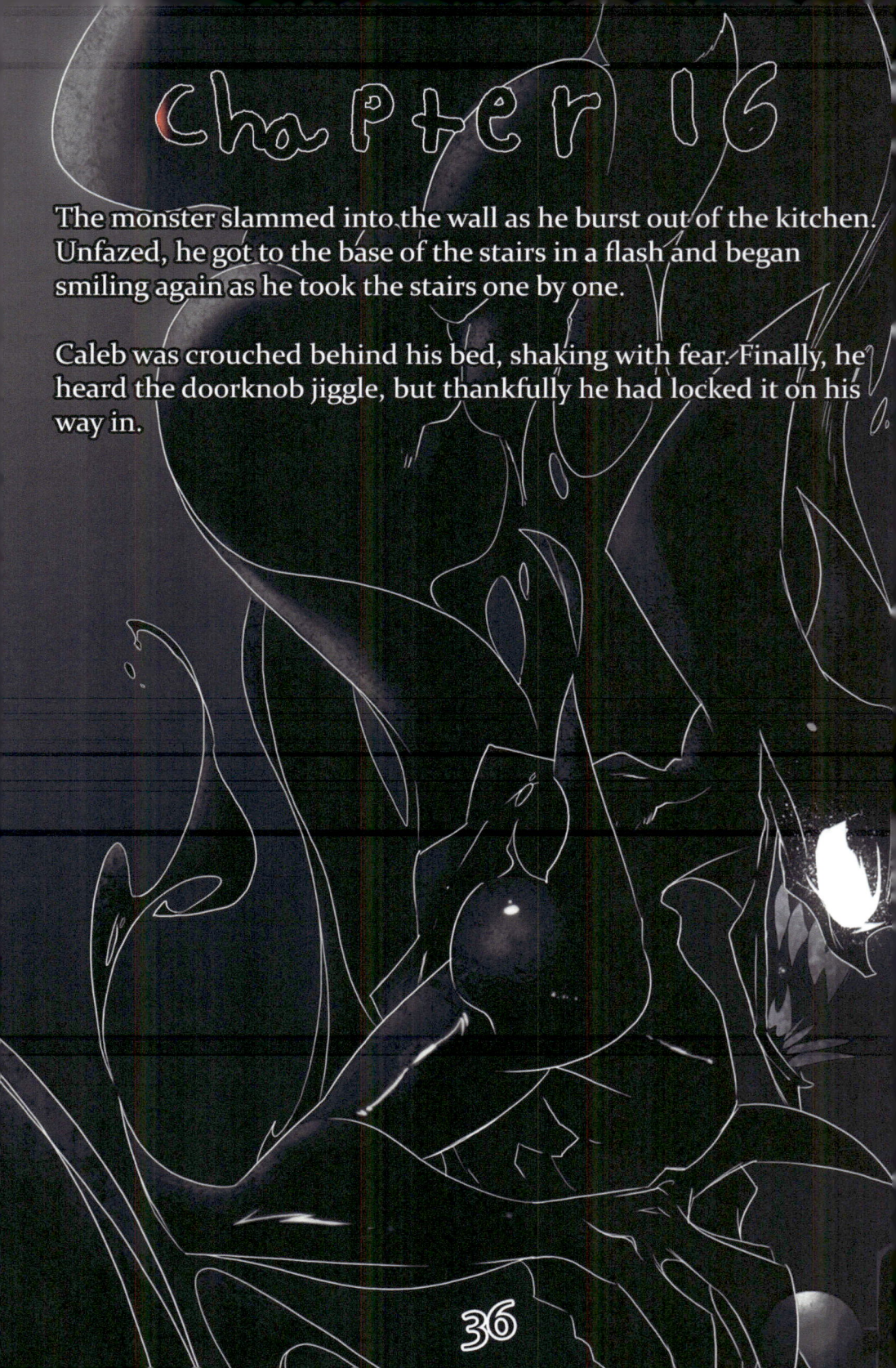

chapter 16

The monster slammed into the wall as he burst out of the kitchen. Unfazed, he got to the base of the stairs in a flash and began smiling again as he took the stairs one by one.

Caleb was crouched behind his bed, shaking with fear. Finally, he heard the doorknob jiggle, but thankfully he had locked it on his way in.

This reminds me of something," Eniko said quietly as he laid his head against the door. "What's that book that always scared you when you were little?" Eniko asked. "The one with the pigs? Ah, I remember the line. I'll huff, and I'll puff…"

Smoke was creeping beneath the door, slowly filling the room. Frantically, Caleb began looking around, trying to figure out what he was going to do, when he saw the window and had an idea.

Puffing, Eniko finished, "…and I'll blow your house down." He roared as he burst through the door. Glancing around, he saw an empty room until his eyes landed on the open window and he saw Caleb's foot slipping out.

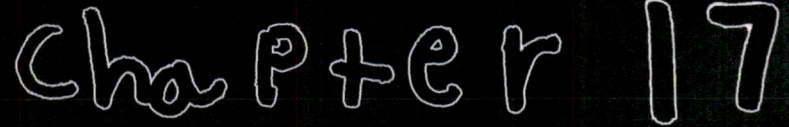

Chapter 17

Once Caleb was on the roof, he rubbed his eyes. A beam of light caught his attention from off in the distance. "Is the garage really so far away?" he whispered. It seemed like a mile, but it was the only place he could think of to hide.

Suddenly, Eniko was at the window, and Caleb ran for the edge as Eniko began fuming. When Caleb jumped, he floated for a moment before slowly falling the ground.

Somehow, Caleb landed on a padded lawn chair and rolled onto his feet. He stood up, confused, and started running toward the garage.

Looking over his shoulder, the window was empty, but Caleb heard a blood-curdling roar. It sounded like a train hitting a building. Every door burst open and all the windows shattered; smoke poured out of every opening and rose above the disappearing house.

The garage didn't seem to be getting closer, and as Caleb ran, the walls looked funny, like they were coming apart. First, the front wall with the garage doors lifted straight up. As Caleb watched in amazement, the other three drifted apart and began rising into the air.

"No, no, no," Caleb thought as he watched the walls vanish into the sky. His hope faded.

chapter 18

Where the building had once stood, there was nothing but a concrete floor. In the center of the building were cans of paint. Caleb thought they were glowing, and he knew what he had to do.

With a quick glance over his shoulder, Caleb saw Eniko floating above him, filling the sky like a cloud, smiling that evil smile.

Caleb rushed for the cans like beacons at the back of the garage. He stumbled into them and grabbed the first one he could, but it was stuck shut. Quickly, he grabbed another one, but the lid wouldn't budge.

"Think, think" Caleb said as he heard Eniko laughing.

Out of the corner of his eye, he saw a screwdriver. Eniko saw it, too, and dived for Caleb. He was a pillar of smoke rushing out of the sky while Caleb fumbled to get the tool under the lid.

Caleb was frantically prying at the lid when he dropped the screwdriver. He knelt down to pick it up again and looked up. Eniko was an enormous wave coming straight for him.

The screwdriver finally caught the edge and he pried it open. Inside, Caleb could see the orange paint glowing. He grabbed it with both hands. Eniko was inches away.

"You want all the colors?" Caleb yelled as he threw the paint into the air. "You can have them!"

The paint hit Eniko square in the face, and he winced in pain as he crashed down on Caleb and exploded into a colorful fog.

Chapter 19

After the cloud disappeared, Caleb rubbed his eyes and looked around. The house was gone, the garage was gone, and the darkness was gone. All around him was a snow-white fog. Up ahead he saw a figure and took a few steps forward. The fog cleared, revealing a vast expanse and a small figure playing in a puddle of paint.

Walking up to it, he saw that it was a purple creature splashing around and rubbing it all over himself. It was one of the happiest things Caleb had ever seen.

When it finally saw Caleb, he froze and put his hands behind his back.

"Hi Caleb," it said, kicking at a purple puddle.

"Hi," Caleb replied, puzzled. "Who are you?"

"You don't remember me?" it responded. It's voice cracked. "I used to be your best friend. We jumped off of the doghouse together. You took me to school in your backpack every day for years."

Looking up, the toy could see that Caleb was still puzzled.

"I was there when you first got Max. I was there when the accident happened and everyone in the town became zombies."

"Neko?" Caleb asked.

Memories from before the town was turned into zombies were hazy and seemed like a million years ago. But as he thought about them more they kept coming.

Going for rides in their red wagon, chasing fireflies...Caleb remembered in a rush and felt sad he had forgotten about him.

46

"That was you?" Caleb asked, surprised. "Eniko?"

The toy looked bashful, "Oh, that's just a name I came up with. Neko is the name I like. I just didn't know how to get your attention, and things got out of hand. I didn't mean to hurt you, or Max or your friends. My anger kept growing and a monster took over. It felt like I was trapped inside and couldn't control what was happening."

"I'm so sorry," Caleb said leaning close to the toy's face. "I'll never forget you again."

From behind Caleb, the unicorn walked up and looked down at the two.

"Did you ever get your toe back on?" the Unicorn asked.

"Yeah," Caleb said as he wiped away a tear. "Wait, what are you doing here?"

"I've come to wake you up," the Unicorn said.

47

"Wake me up from what?" Caleb asked as he looked around. Neko was still standing there, but where the purple puddle had been before, it was now pale white.

Looking up, Caleb saw Neko and the unicorn floating away,

"Why am I floating?" Caleb asked looking down. Nothing was underneath his feet.

"You're dreaming, Caleb," Neko said quietly.

"Close your eyes, Caleb," the Unicorn replied.

"Where can I find you?" Caleb asked as darkness crept over and his eyes softly closed.

"Someplace you always see but never look," was the fading response that echoed through the darkness.

Chapter 20

When Caleb opened his eyes, he was lying back in his bed. Once he sat up, he didn't know where he was. The room looked strange with sunlight beaming in. Everything was hazy. Caleb rubbed his eyes sleepily and realized he was in his room, but couldn't remember going to sleep the night before.

"What happened? I feel like I ran a hundred miles last night," Caleb said half awake.

Suddenly, the dream came back: Eniko, his parents, the town going back to black and white, Max. Caleb's eyes were alert now as he searched frankily for his dog. He finally caught a glimpse of Max sleeping next to his bed and let out a sigh of relief. Caleb hopped out of bed and gave Max a big hug.

"Neko," Caleb whispered remembering more details from his dream.

"Max, get up. Have you seen Neko?"

Max started sniffing around the room as Caleb went over to his bed and looked under it.

"Where could he be?" Caleb said, looking in his closet.

After looking in the toy chest, underneath his desk and in the pile of toys his mom had told him to clean up, Caleb didn't think he would ever find him, when Max let out a "woof" by the dresser.

Caleb walked over and looked down. Peeking out from underneath the dresser was the unpainted arm of his one-time favorite toy.

Bending down, Caleb pulled the toy out and brought him up to his face.

"I knew I'd find you." He said to Neko.

Downstairs he could hear his mom making breakfast so Caleb put on his slippers, went downstairs and started heading for the garage.

"Caleb, what are you still doing in your pajamas, don't you remember what day it is," his mom asked.

"Oh, I remember" Caleb, replied. "I just have to take care of something I forgot to do."

"Don't take too long, you still have to get ready," his mom called as Caleb walked out the front door.

Jake and Nola were just crossing into Caleb's yard as he stepped outside.

"What are you doing?" Nola asked as they came up beside him.

"Catching up with an old friend. I had the strangest dream about him last night," Caleb said. "Somehow I forgot to paint him. Want to come help? I have a few extra brushes in the garage."

"Yea!" Jake and Nola replied.

They walked into the garage, and grabbed some brushes and buckets of paint.

The kids painted Neko with all the colors they could.

"Caleb, bring your friends in here and get ready, we have to go" Caleb's mom yelled from inside.

"Come on guys, he isn't going anywhere," Caleb said.

"Why are you smiling?" Nola asked.

"Nothing, I was just thinking about a dream I had last night" Caleb replied.

As they walked out of the garage Caleb glanced back over his shoulder to catch one last look at Neko.

"Glad to have you back Neko" Caleb said softly to himself, "I wish we could talk like in my dream..."

As the lifeless doll sat there Caleb walked back into the house with his friends but not before doing one last double take as he could have sworn Neko gave a tiny wink at him.

The End.

You've made it to the end but there's still more to do. See if you can find the 8 hidden items found in this book to answer these 8 questions:

1) Can you find the name of the town?

2) Zach drew the pictures for this book and is a real cat lover. Can you find his cat?

3) Can you find an area code hidden in this book? Where is it from?

4) The Golden Driller is somewhere in these pages, where is he and what town is he from?

5) There are three posters of classic horror films, what are they?

6) What's the punchline for this joke:
What does it take to be a zombie?
(The answer is hidden in this book)

7) Can you find one of the characters from our next book?
Hint: he is made of yarn...

8) Witches use a book of spells called a Necronomicon, where is it hidden?

*Bonus:

-What other book that you find objects in use the same color scheme as Calebs magnifying glass handle?

For the real Caleb, may you always keep your playful heart.

Love,

Dad (Steven)

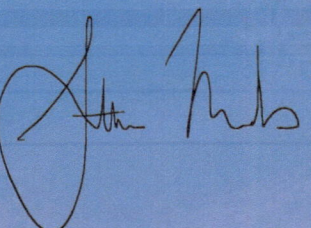

This book is dedicated to my daughter, the real Nola, may her life be as colorful as her dreams.

Love,

Dad (Isaac)

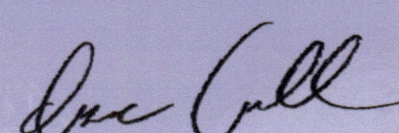

I'm a full time artist from Tulsa Oklahoma. I started off drawing at a young age but didn't pursue it as a career until after high school. At the time my main interest was film making and I still hope to do that as well in the future. Most likely in the form of animation.

Zach Raw

Answer Page

Congratulations, hopefully you found everything. If you still need some help, here are the answers and a little back story.

1. Eidolon. Page 18.

2. His cat is on page 14.

3. 303 is on the side of Caleb's desk on page 5. It is from Denver, Colorado and it is where the author lives.

4. The Golden Driller is from Tulsa, Oklahoma and he can be found on page 52. The producer and artist live in Tulsa, too.

5. "Heckraiser," "Four Forks" (Page 37) and "Night of the Living Zombies." (Page 50)

6. Dead'ication. Found on the Teachers chalkboard on Page 26.

7. On page 50. Its the Bear, keep an eye out for him.

8. Page 22.

9. Bonus: Where's Waldo.

www.ingramcontent.com/pod-product-compliance
Lightning Source LLC
Chambersburg PA
CBHW040744250626
47164CB00006BA/166